KITTY and KAT
Pet Peeves

BY ROBERT BEALS III

Illustrations by Blueberry Illustrations

BOOK 5: KITTY AND KAT ADVENTURE SERIES
PUBLISHER: SELF-PUBLISHED,
EDMOND, OKLAHOMA, USA

Illustrations by Blueberry Illustrations

ISBN: 978-1-7351386-3-3

DEDICATED TO MY SISTER KAT

This was your idea from the beginning.
Thank you!

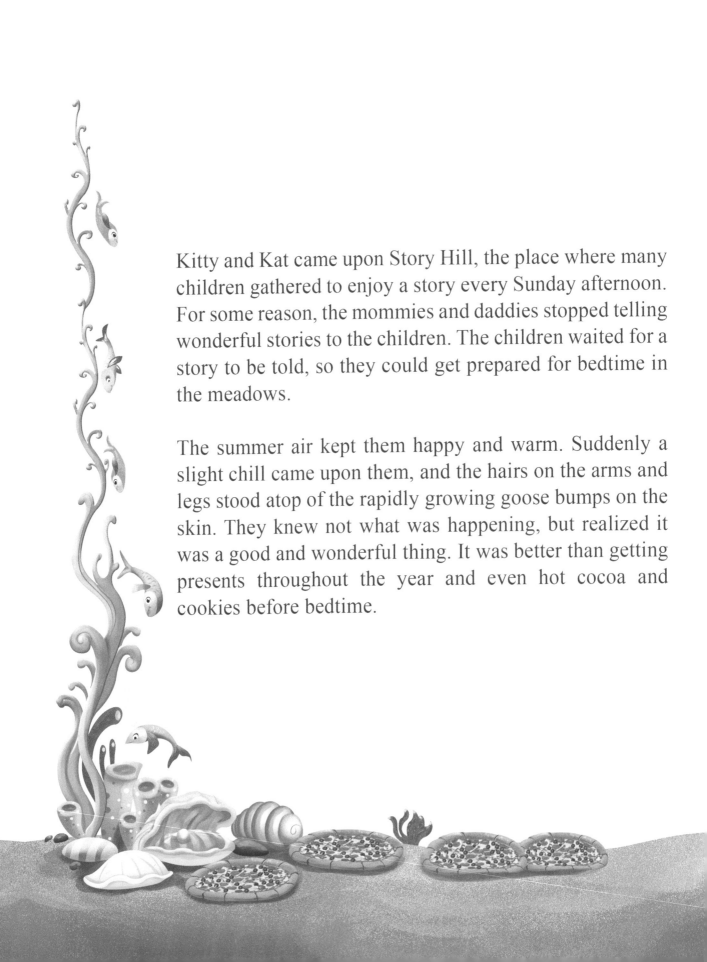

Kitty and Kat came upon Story Hill, the place where many children gathered to enjoy a story every Sunday afternoon. For some reason, the mommies and daddies stopped telling wonderful stories to the children. The children waited for a story to be told, so they could get prepared for bedtime in the meadows.

The summer air kept them happy and warm. Suddenly a slight chill came upon them, and the hairs on the arms and legs stood atop of the rapidly growing goose bumps on the skin. They knew not what was happening, but realized it was a good and wonderful thing. It was better than getting presents throughout the year and even hot cocoa and cookies before bedtime.

PurrAnimal was the cause of the chill and the fantastic feeling that surrounded them. The great protector, as known by all, came to help the children today, by reading out to them a story.

He flew from the sky and landed by the kids. They were very excited, as they knew that PurrAnimal was a great and friendly beast. He protected all the animals and children from harm throughout the world. It was finally time for the story they had been waiting for—*Pet Peeves*!

The story begins.

Kitty and Kat were walking down the road,
Passing by their friends, the frog and toad.
Continuing toward the hound and dog,
Still sitting upon the big fat log.

They remembered the animal pairs from their first journey when trying to look for mice for their mommies. They also recalled some of the animals they met while they were questing for Squint in their second journey.

Along the way, in this adventure, Kitty and Kat met Ant and Flea in the big ole tree. PurrAnimal continued, "The tree was very tall, and Kitty and Kat could not see the top through all the branches and leaves." There were many branches, leaves, and different areas of the tree for the animals to live comfortably together. A leader was selected for each branch to ensure that all the animals—spiders, birds, squirrels, and even Ant and Flea—played nicely all the time. Ant and Flea rarely came down from their gigantic home.

"Hey, Ant and Flea, "why don't you come down from your tree and play with us today?" asked Kat. They said that they were too afraid of their aunt and uncle. Their aunt was upset that she could not find her pet, Peeves. Flea had invited Peeves to stay over and play with all the animal friends up in the tree. Having played throughout the night, Peeves, Ant, and Flea all had finally fallen asleep.

When they woke up the next morning, Peeves was gone! Ant and Flea searched and searched for three days straight, but he remained missing. That was three weeks ago! No wonder Aunt Chovie was so upset.

Peeves was a huge ugly pet with two heads and two antennae on each head. Its bright green body was covered with clothes that were never washed. That is why Peeves was called "dirty laundry." His big fat belly always stuck out under his shirt. He was very smelly, with that big ole belly. He had four legs, and he wore different-colored tennis shoes.

Ant said, "Come on up and we'll show you where Peeves was last. That could give us a clue as to where he might be now." As Kitty and Kat climbed the tree, they reached the third branch. It extended three times farther than any other branch and was about to break because it was so large and heavy.

Many barrels, left by pigs, were tied to this branch and so they were called pork barrels. This branch was called the "Le-jee" branch and was run by Polly Tics. Polly tried very hard to make sure that all the animals played well together, but it was an impossible task. Many of them fell off the branch into the swamp below.

There were 96 areas on this branch, again three times more than normal. The name of each area was written on the tree. This was done so that the animals could keep track of where they were in the branch community.

As they traveled down the branch, they came to a place between Area 50 and Area 52.

There they met Ant's best friend, Marsha the Martian. "Hey," "why do they call you Marsha?" asked Kat. "Probably because I marsh a lot," she said. They really needed friends that could marsh a lot while trying to find Aunt Chovie's pet, Peeves.

Aunt Chovie was also kind of smelly, and that is why she did not mind being around her pet, Peeves. She looked like a slimy slender fish and loved jumping on pizzas all day, just to confuse the humans. She and Uncle Chovie both did this for fun.

Now all the animals, along with Marsha the Martian, came down from the tree in hopes to find Peeves, so that Aunt Chovie would no longer be mad. Arriving at the bottom, Ant and Flea thought it looked like such a small world without the perch of the branches above. Nonetheless, they continued to look for Peeves.

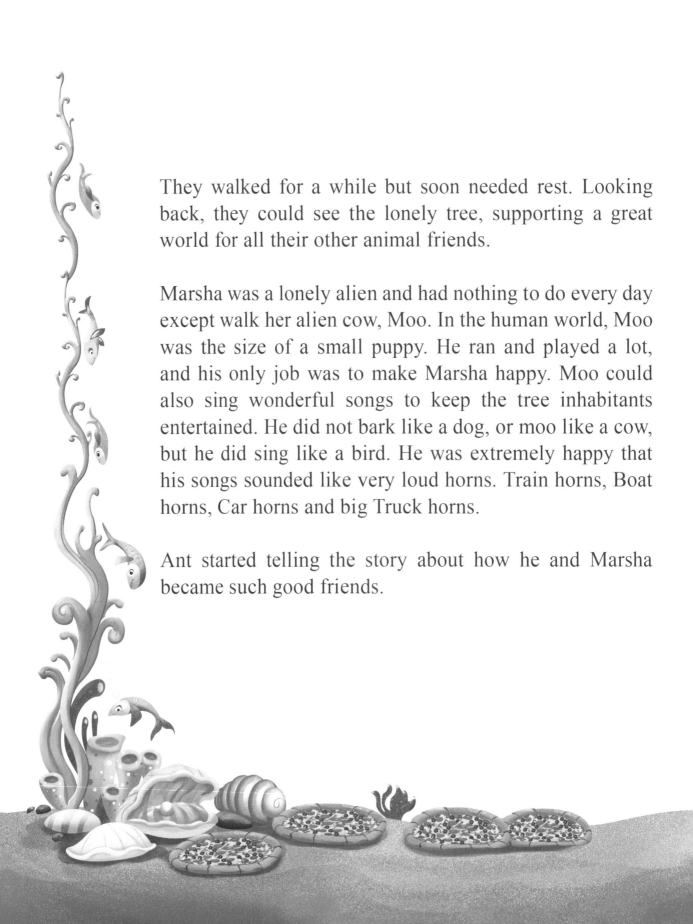

They walked for a while but soon needed rest. Looking back, they could see the lonely tree, supporting a great world for all their other animal friends.

Marsha was a lonely alien and had nothing to do every day except walk her alien cow, Moo. In the human world, Moo was the size of a small puppy. He ran and played a lot, and his only job was to make Marsha happy. Moo could also sing wonderful songs to keep the tree inhabitants entertained. He did not bark like a dog, or moo like a cow, but he did sing like a bird. He was extremely happy that his songs sounded like very loud horns. Train horns, Boat horns, Car horns and big Truck horns.

Ant started telling the story about how he and Marsha became such good friends.

One day, Ant was walking far out on the tree branch when he fell. Marsha's Moo just happened to be on the ground below. He was playing and having fun. Ant landed on Moo's back. Startled and confused, Moo sprung off running with Ant on his back, just like a cowboy riding a bull. This was a day when Marsha was not holding the leash on her friend.

Marsha whistled for Moo and the sound of a loud horn from a big truck filled the air. Moo stopped and walked back to Marsha with the startled passenger aboard. Ant and Marsha were now best friends ever, because she had saved him from the accidental ride on her alien cow.

The team continued resting for a while. Unknown to them, Pet Peeves was magically transforming on the other side of the hill. He now looked like an anchovy wearing a red hat. He happened to be living with the anchovies for so long that he had eventually turned into one.

PurrAnimal had just finished reading that part of the book, when suddenly, over the hill, came 25,000 sets of white eyes, 12,000 pairs of white teeth, and the pitter-patter of 25,000 pairs of tiny little anchovy feet.

There were 12,000 Aunt Chovies running fast toward Ant, Flea, Kitty, Kat, and Marsha. They were running so fast that Ant could not keep up. "Come faster," said Kat. "Real fast," said Kitty. "Ant has bubble gum on his shoes!" said Flea.

Poor little Ant's shoes stuck to the ground and he could not keep up with everyone.

PurrAnimal then took to the air,
Flying so fast, as not to despair,
Chucked a thousand pizzas onto the ground,
For all Aunt Chovies to start to surround,
The pizzas, not Ant, while still on the ground.

The chaos was over, as it winded down. Pet Peeves had transformed into another Aunt Chovie and was caught in the crowd on top of the pizzas. Aunt Chovie could tell it was him because of the red hat. She met the new anchovy and no longer had a Pet Peeve. She finally realized how happy she was, because there were no Pet Peeves left. They could all finally live happily ever after.

ENTRANCE TO BOOK - 6
PERILS OF PET PIG PINKY

JUST A NOTE ON HOW THIS BOOK

came about. I was working on Quest for Squint, on the part where pet pig Pinky talked about perfectly preposterous pet peeves. My sister said, "Hey, you should have a book called Pet Peeves!" So, a book title was born.

I was thinking about how folks having pet peeves may lead to differences within families. I thought if we could get rid of people's pet peeves, the world might become a better place. There would be less anxiety and frustration in everyday life. It would be a good lesson to learn as a child.

Aunt Chovie and Uncle Chovie come from my son. He
honestly was concerned why we had only anchovies and no
uncle chovies on pizzas. He was just a small child at the time,
and this was a perfectly innocent statement. And totally hilarious.

Marsha the Martian comes from when my siblings and I were younger.
We created stories and recorded them like a podcast. We did the
sound on sound recording with a different track at a slower speed.
When replayed at regular speed, it sounded like a chipmunk-type
Martian voice. And Moo is the name of my sister's cat today.

So, there is a little bit of all of us in here!

Hope you and your family enjoy the book.

Thanks,
GrampaBuddy

BORN IN NEW LONDON, CONNECTICUT,

part of a military family, Robert Beals III lived in many places
as a child. He had early success in storytelling and creation
of poems and papers for elementary school projects.

Beals published four of five books and continues to write:

MiceQuest
Quest for Squint
BatButts
DuckQuackle (in works)
Pet Peeves

"His second book in the Kitty and Kat adventure series,
Quest for Squint, is based on one of his favorite poems
about a wolfman, which he wrote when he was a child."

Beals currently resides in Edmond, Oklahoma, USA.
He loves children, animals, and some people too!

CPSIA information can be obtained
at www.ICGtesting.com
Printed in the USA
LVHW072119270720
661634LV00011B/296